My Sister Lotta and Me

by **Helena Dahlbäck**

retold by **Rika Lesser**

pictures by Charlotte Ramel

Henry Holt and Company / New York

For Johanna

—R. L.

Henry Holt and Company, Inc.
Publishers since 1866
115 West 18th Street
New York, New York 10011

Henry Holt is a registered
trademark of Henry Holt and Company, Inc.

First published in the United States in 1993
by Henry Holt and Company, Inc.
Published in Canada by Fitzhenry & Whiteside Ltd.,
195 Allstate Parkway, Markham, Ontario L3R 4T8.
Originally published in Sweden in 1991
by Bonniers Juniorförlag under *Min syster Lotta och jag*.

Library of Congress Catalog Card Number: 93-78135
ISBN: 0-8050-2558-8
First American Edition—1993
Printed in Belgium

1 3 5 7 9 10 8 6 4 2

I have a sister, and her name is Lotta.
She's lots of fun. I'm sure you'd like to meet her.

Lotta and I play together every day.
We're not just sisters, we're best friends.

My sister and I show our colors all the time.
Lotta is red and I, myself, am blue.

She's red as a heart,
red as a fire engine.
I'm blue as a bluebonnet,
blue as our cat's blue ribbon.

At bathtime anyone can see:
I'm like a willow, Lotta's like a pillow.

Lotta's stomach simply won't stay in.

Mine may pop out now and then…
but it's plainly nothing like hers.
Some tummies come as outies,
and they plump up, like Lotta's.

Silky and thick, Lotta's hair keeps on going.
Wiry and thin, mine seems to have stopped
   growing.

If hers gets any longer, she'll have to climb
   something higher—
maybe a ladder, maybe even a tower—to
   let down all that hair.

We planned a party for a secret friend.

Mom helped me bake the cake.
Lotta prepared the goody bags and wrapped
the presents.
We hung balloons and strung up decorations.

But we forgot to send the invitations!

When we play school, I'm always the teacher.
Lotta, she's a classroom full of children—
the most mischievous class I've ever had.

There may be only one of her,
but suddenly she's everywhere.

Behind our house, beneath an old oak tree,
we found a jewel box filled with earth and buried things.

In Lotta's hands, all things come to life:

A skull and bones—tiny, pincushion-sized—
becomes a mouse, or even several mice.

To them our cat (remember our kitten?)
is terrifying: a huge, hungry lion!

Lotta is fearless.
She goes around for hours with her eyes shut.
Me, I'm chicken. I can't even watch her.

If Lotta can't see danger, she's not scared.
I'm brave when it's quite clear there's
    nothing there.

I've tried to show her how to crack eggs and
    beat them,
but Lotta claps them hard between her hands,
then lets them fall like little Humpty-Dumpties!

"Don't bounce your chick eggs or they will
    crack!" I scream.
And she shrieks back, "Too many bakers ruin
    the honey buns!"

Sometimes we quarrel, leave everything in
	the middle,
and we clam up, pretend to watch TV.

After a while, nobody can remember:
What did I say? What did she say?

After a while, one of us says she's sorry,
we start to smile, and everything's okay.

When she makes up, hearts go flying,
and any day could be Saint Valentine's.
Sometimes I wish I were, but I'm not like her:
I like to like, while Lotta loves to love.

If you're nearby she'll cover you with kisses.
And if you're not she'll send you ooo's and xxx's.

This may seem strange, but
Lotta's afraid of the dark!
We can't go to sleep before I swear
that I've searched the entire house,
and there are no ghosts anywhere:

      not in our closet

      not under the chair

      and certainly not in our little bed

      where only the two of us fit.

Every night I tell her this, and then
and only then
do we fall fast asleep.